Crocs

By Mary-Margaret Patterson

S2 Press
Bethesda, MD

First Edition

To obtain more copies or make bulk purchases you may also contact the publisher at:

S2 Press
9006 Friars Rd
Bethesda, MD 20187
United States
301-493-4982
socrtwo@s2services.com
s2press.com

First Printing: 2014

Library of Congress Control Number: 2014947214
ISBN 978-1-5006943-1-9

Cover photo by Molly Blythe Teichert
Watermark/frame photo by Lynn Friedman
Shoe photo used for front cover frame
by Donald Townsend

For Emmett and Tucker
and boys just like you half a world away

Table of Contents

Chapter One

My Old Shoes

"Ow! Ow!" I cried. My Crocs, my wonderful, comfortable rubbery shoes were pushing on my big toes. They were biting me. Stabbing me on the very ends of my biggest toes. How could they?

It felt like I stubbed my toe. But it didn't go away.

"Ow! Ow!" I said again. I was running. I looked down on the familiar yellow shoes I was so proud of. Noticed the holes on top that let in the cool air on this summer day. Looked at the dried mud on the rippled bottoms that had kept my feet dry, more or less, the last time it rained.

"You're just growing; they're way too small," Mom said. "You'll need a new pair. And so will your brother."

She threw them on a pile of outgrown tennis shoes in the closet along with the hot pink Crocs shoes my brother had worn that day. There were seven pairs of too small tennis shoes in the pile already. The Crocs made nine pairs. I counted them.

The next day Mom bought us clean, new, bigger Crocs. We put them on right away. A bright orange pair for me and a green pair for my brother. I forgot about my yellow ones until I saw Mom tossing them in a shopping bag with the other old shoes.

"Where are you going with our shoes?" I asked her, spying my yellow Crocs on top.

"You can't wear these anymore. They're too small," she said. "So I'm taking them to Gramma to give to the church for kids who need them. OK?"

"Yeah, I guess so." Who would want these old shoes, I wondered? They were awful dirty anyway. And smelly. One of the tennis shoes had an entire hole where my brother's big toe went all the way through. I had seen Mom throw some like them in the trash with banana peels and egg shells, and more stinky things. Well, that's the last I'll hear of my yellow Crocs, I thought. I said a silent, sad good-bye to them. They had been good Crocs.

Chapter Two

Gramma and Her Washer

At her house, Gramma dumped all the shoes into her washing machine with lots of soap and hot water. Then she laid them out in the sun to dry. They were still old, but they didn't smell anymore. The yellow Crocs came out nice and bright. They looked almost new. But Gramma told me later she had to throw away the pair of tennis shoes with the hole completely out the front of the shoe. Nobody could wear *that* shoe. Even a very poor kid wouldn't want that one, I guess.

When the other shoes were all dry, she tied each pair together with strong string. Now there were eight pairs of old, but clean, kids' shoes. She dropped them off at the church on a mound of other used kid shoes.

Well, that's the last we'll hear of those, she thought and dusted off her hands.

* * *

The yellow Crocs got practically covered up when some other folks added more old shoes to the pile. It got a lot darker around the Crocs. Then came a day when they were squashed into a very small space in a big old suitcase with plaid sides. It got zipped up tight. There was no cool air coming in the air holes then. The yellow Crocs could hardly breathe at all. It was pitch black. So they went to sleep with all the other shoes.

Chapter Three

The Longest Journey

Across the wide ocean to the East

and across the world's biggest, hottest,

driest desert where it never rains and

across a jungle where it rains all the time. And over some mountains with snow on top and across a huge lake. Then down in a farm town in Africa, another boy sits by the side of a dusty red dirt road.

The boy is seven years old. Most days he goes to school. It's a long walk. It takes about an hour, but he doesn't mind that. There are other kids to walk with. It can be fun. Sometimes they sing a little. Or kick a stone along the way before them. Other times they look up and see a tiny silver airplane sweep across the sky. Going some place. Maybe some place really big like a city with people everywhere. Certainly not Shikokho, his village in Kenya where fewer than 3,000 people live.

When it rains in the village, things are different. It can rain really hard. Sometimes rain comes for day and days. Then, Tumaini, for that is his name, doesn't go to school. The mud is too deep and slippery on the red dirt roads. He might skid to his knees and get his school clothes plastered with mud. Granny didn't like that; then she had to wash his clothes again in the river and beat them on stones to get them clean and lay them out later to dry in the sun.

On a rainy walk to school, Tumaini might step on a sharp stick he can't see in the goo. Or scrape his foot on a rough rock until it bleeds. (That happened more than once.) Or squish a worm. Or get bitten on his toe by a spider or-- shudder--even a snake hiding in the mud--just a very little snake. For Tumaini has no shoes.

A lot of the other children can't go to school when it rains either. About half the kids in the village school don't have shoes. If you have flip flops, sometimes you can go in the rain, if the roads aren't too bad. "But it sure slows you down," Tumaini thought.

He complained to his Granny that he had no shoes.

"I was angry because I had no shoes," his Granny replied, in her best story-telling voice. "Then I saw a man who had NO FEET!" She went back to hoeing their corn in her big brown bare feet.

After that, Tumaini didn't say anything to her about shoes anymore.

He actually liked feeling his bare feet on the smooth dirt floor of his home. It was cool and out of the sun and dry when it rained. And he was used to playing outside in his bare feet, like boys everywhere.

But he still wished he had just one pair of shoes. Then he wouldn't miss school when it rained.

He dreamed that if he had shoes, he could get one of the prizes for perfect attendance. He wouldn't be behind in his lessons. So he would be there to play football with the other boys in the school yard every single day at recess. He loved to run and run with them after that black and white ball. (This is the same game that American kids call soccer.) Most of all, he wouldn't miss lunch, when he could eat his fill of beans and ugali—the cornmeal mush everybody eats all the time in Shikokho. That fills up your tummy so it doesn't rumble so much.

Chapter Four

"Something for You"

One day when Tumaini was at school, the foreign doctor came. The class lined up and sang for him, to welcome him all the way from America. He heard that the doctor came to their country in a big airplane. Maybe it was one of those silver jets sliding through the clouds high up in the bright blue sky. But, the doctor arrived in their village in an old van with big dirty wheels. He always had several suitcases.

Then all the boys and girls lined up and bared their arms for a shot. "Aiyaaya!" ("Ow!") Teacher said it would help keep them from getting sick. Everybody Tumaini knew got sick from something off and on, all the time. Even he did, sometimes.

After the shot, they each got a piece of hard candy for being brave. But, it didn't really hurt, not near as much as the last time Tumaini scraped the side of his foot bloody on a jagged rock on the road walking to school. (And it wasn't even raining that day!)

* * *

After he got his candy, one of the village women pulled him to the side.

"We may have something for you," she said. "Go stand in line with those other boys over there."

A teacher was rummaging in a big plaid suitcase that lay zipped open on a table. What a surprise! She was handing out shoes for children to try on.

They looked like pretty good shoes. They weren't new, but there were Nikes and Reeboks and Keds. Some had Velcro straps that went "ripppp" when you undid them. Some had laces to tie. At least one pair had soles that winked and blinked red or green lights on the sides! (Tumaini wanted those. But somebody else got them.)

By the time Tumaini reached the table, most of the shoes were gone. Only some rubbery shoes were left. He started to feel disappointed. (Just his luck!) Then the woman handed him a pair of bright yellow rubbery shoes with holes across the top and ridges on the soles.

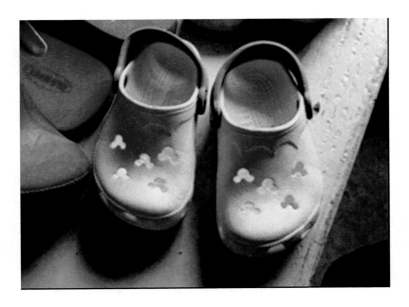

"You can try these," she said. They were a little big, but they stayed on with the strap snapped tight. (It's ok to have shoes a *little* big when you are still growing, he thought.)

Tumaini didn't know if he could run in them, but when the teacher wasn't watching, he tried and he could. They even felt a little bouncy. On the long walk home the air came in to cool his hot, dusty feet.

Best of all, the next time it rained, Tumaini went to school. The water came in just a little bit through the air holes, but the bottoms of his feet were fine. He wiped the shoes off at school, lined them up against the wall to dry before the walk home.

"Crocs" they said on the back. "Short for crocodiles," his teacher said with a smile. Of course, they weren't crocodiles; Tumaini knew what THOSE were! But it made him feel kind of powerful to call them Crocs, after crocodiles.

He wore them all through English class. (In schools in Kenya, children learn English because Kenya was a British colony, long ago before independence.)

Tumaini also wore his yellow Crocs to the football field; he wore them to lunch every day and to church on Sunday. Even when it rained.

Chapter Five

Back in America

Back on the other side of the world, in America, I went to second grade and my brother went to first. When it is warm outside, we like to run around the yard in our bare feet on the green grass and soft moss. We can sneak up on each other very quietly that way. (Boo!)

But to go to school we wear ordinary shoes. And for soccer practice, we have special soccer shoes. Evenings and weekends, we have Crocs. This year we wore our new Crocs. (Of course, they weren't really new anymore; got scuffed up a bit and kind of dirty whenever it rained outside. But all you have to do is wash them off.)

After school, I like to play with my Mom's iPhone where I can read messages from Dad when he is away. My brother plays games on her iPhone. He could sit there FOREVER!

We can play on the iPhone a lot if we are sick and have to stay home from school. But we are almost never sick.

Sometimes we get e-mails on our computer from our Gramma even though she only lives 15 minutes away, by car.

One day, however, an old-fashioned letter came addressed to us. It slipped through the mail slot in our front door. It had a funny-looking stamp on it.

My brother and I NEVER get old-fashioned "snail" mail. Mom said the envelope was postmarked in Ny-Robe-Ee (Nairobi). She said that is the capital city of a country called Kenya, in East Africa. We had to look it up on a map on the Internet. That letter sure came a long way and as slow as a snail; it was mailed WEEKS ago! It was printed in pencil. And this is what it said:

Dear Emmett and Tucker,

My name is Tumaini. I am seven. I live in Shikokho.

Did you give me my shoes? A doctor gave out shoes at school. We had to write a thank you. I got your name out of a hat.

My shoes are yellow. Crocodiles. I go to school in them. Didn't have shoes before. I play football. Do you?

Your friend,

Tumaini

Later, we found out Tumaini means "hope" in another language. That's what the Internet said. Maybe we could send him an e-mail sometime? Or another pair of shoes next year? Tumaini must be growing too.

The End

Afterword

Although Tumaini's story is fiction, it reflects life from a child's perspective in Shikokho, a densely populated farming village of 3,000 persons located in the hills of Western Province, Kenya, just north of Lake Victoria near the Ugandan border. The collection of children's shoes for distribution there continues at Chevy Chase Presbyterian Church in Washington, DC. The church has helped organize and support development projects in this isolated village since 1989 when church activist Gretchen Hobbs Donaldson returned from fieldwork there for her master's degree in international education at American University.

A women's self-help group she lived and worked with in Shikokho partnered with representatives of the church. Over the years, this collaboration resulted initially in the construction and stocking of the region's first medical clinic, maternity wing and staff housing. A doctor from the Chevy Chase congregation visits every other year now and works in cooperation with the clinic's Kenyan-trained nurse. The clinic in this overwhelmingly Christian village of many denominations is nonprofit, nonsectarian and open to all.

Groups of church members and friends have visited Shikokho ten times to date aiding in many projects including: electrification beginning with solar cookers, planting trees, introducing rabbit husbandry for food and tea growing for a cash crop, helping in the school and library and, most recently, drilling an artesian well which now provides a safe, steady water source to supplement eight local springs which are being renovated to correct contamination and silt-clogging. Church members also distribute mosquito nets, contribute to micro-finance projects, fund elementary and secondary scholarships and pay for some textbooks. They recently gave the school its first computers. Local women receive donated pay for sewing required school uniforms on manual sewing machines using fabric provided by the program. Contributions also help sustain the village's recently organized orphan feeding and day care program which provides one meal daily to over 150 children who have lost one or both parents, often to the Africa-wide AIDS epidemic.

Crocs

I wrote the "Crocs" story for my two grandsons who contributed their outgrown shoes for the first campaign for used shoes for Shikokho. It was only in 2011 that Dr. Jim Shelhamer first took shoes to Shikokho because it bothered him that so many children lacked shoes of any kind. Because they walk everywhere barefoot, many Shikikho children contract hookworm parasites that can lead to malnutrition and other health problems.

Dr. Shelhamer started to address this need by giving away 50 pairs of used kids' shoes collected at the church and packed into a suitcase; 75% were rubbery shoes such as Crocs, which are made of a material that doesn't rot. "They protect the whole foot, as opposed to flip-flops. So they protect and endure better than leather or cloth shoes," he says. The next time he went to Shikokho, in 2013, he took 100 pairs of shoes and plans to take more on his next trip. Delivery and customs difficulties make shipping impractical to such a remote village, volunteers have found. They prefer to take as many as they can pack and carry.

Although this book can be read to young children of almost any age, it is a "chapter" book intended for beginning readers because my grandsons were just learning to read at the time it was written. I was inspired to write it because in their comfortable Washington, DC, lives, the boys come into contact with few, if any, truly economically disadvantaged children. Nor could they comprehend the needs endemic to those growing up in a poor area of a developing country. I hope they, and now others, can begin to understand not only the gulf between the Third World and life in America in the 21st Century, but what individuals can do about it. I believe it helps to know that just because a child has very little, looks and dresses differently and lives in a poor country far away does not detract from his worth as a unique person and potential friend.

* * *

The author will donate the proceeds from the sale of this book to benefit the Shikokho programs supported by the Chevy Chase Presbyterian Church.

To make a direct contribution, send a bank check made out to the church with "for Shikokho" in the notation section of the check. The mailing address is: Chevy Chase Presbyterian Church; One Chevy Chase Circle, N.W.; Washington, DC 20015. The church is a 501(c)(3) organization approved as tax exempt under the Internal Revenue Code of the United States.

Acknowledgments

No book, however brief, sees the light of day without help from many sources. So I thank all the earliest readers of this tiny tale that grew out of a pile of outgrown kids' shoes. Some even tried out this story on young readers-to-be in their own families. Appreciation for this and for sharing many photos taken in Shikokho goes to: Gretchen Hobbs Donaldson, Ellen Jacknain and Jim Shelhamer, M.D. In addition, Barbara Howell, Bonnie Norman, and Scott and Alix Patterson were early readers and photographers.

I owe a debt of gratitude to the late Professor Lowell Ragatz who first introduced me to African history and the needs and significance of the developing world. I especially thank the African children who appear anonymously in photos in the book and who serve as models for this work of fiction.

Paul D. Pruitt's expertise and good suggestions were invaluable. Special thanks go to the Rev. Molly Blythe Teichert not only for her Shikokho photos but for her insistence that this story be published. Finally, thanks to my husband, David S. Patterson, always my first critic and best friend.

Mary-Margaret Patterson
Chevy Chase, Maryland
November 2014

About the Author

Mary-Margaret Sharp Patterson has a background as a staff writer for metropolitan daily newspapers in Chicago and Houston. In Washington, DC, she has worked as a writer and editor for national nonprofits in the fields of the environment, aging and credit union services and has taught journalism at several universities. She has master's and bachelor's degrees from The Ohio State University.